R. A. DICKEY

WITH MICHAEL KAROUNOS

KNUCKLEBALL NED

To Sam —
Happy Reading!

illustrated by **TIM BOWERS**

Tim Bowers

2015

DIAL BOOKS FOR YOUNG READERS ✦ AN IMPRINT OF PENGUIN GROUP (USA) LLC

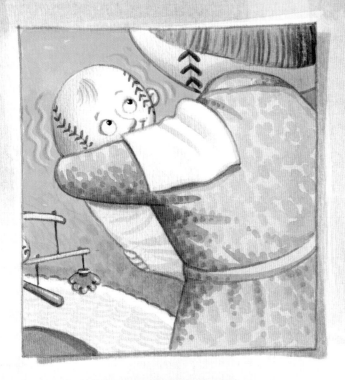

To my four precious knuckleballs,
M.G., Lila, Eli, and Van.
May you always celebrate what
makes you unique.

R.A.D.

To Herb Hartman

T.B.

DIAL BOOKS FOR YOUNG READERS • Published by the Penguin Group • Penguin Group (USA) LLC
375 Hudson Street, New York, New York 10014

USA / Canada / UK / Ireland / Australia / New Zealand / India / South Africa / China
penguin.com
A Penguin Random House Company

Text copyright © 2014 by R. A. Dickey
Pictures copyright © 2014 by Tim Bowers

Cataloging-in-Publication Data is available.

Manufactured in China on acid-free paper
10 9 8 7 6 5 4 3 2 1

Designed by Jasmin Rubero
Text set in Napoleone Slab ITC Std

The publisher does not have any control over and does not assume
any responsibility for author or third-party websites or their content.

The illustrations for this book were painted with acrylic paint on watercolor board, starting with loose color washes and finishing with opaque details. Tone was airbrushed on the heads of the characters to create a rounded baseball-shape effect.

For as long as he could remember, Ned wobbled.

He wobbled when he brushed his teeth,

and when he bumped
his way to the closet for his shoes.

When Ned bumped the shelf, all his toys
came tumbling down on his head.

In the kitchen, he bumped into the refrigerator, and his mom asked, "Are you excited about your first day of school, Ned?"

"I'm nervous," he replied.

"You'll have fun and make lots of friends. You'll see. Just be yourself! Everyone will like you once they get to know you."

Then Ned went outside to wait for the bus.

When the school bus arrived and the doors opened, Ned wobbled down the aisle looking for a seat. He couldn't help bumping into the fastballs and curveballs and sliders sitting in the bus.

"Hey! Watch it!" someone shouted.

Then Ned bumped into the biggest ball he had ever seen. He had a big smile to match. "There's not much room, but you can sit next to me. I'm **SAMMY THE SOFTBALL**, and my mom says I'm the biggest ball of all," said Sammy.

"I'm Ned, and I don't know what kind of ball I am," replied Ned.

"Well, whatever kind of ball you are, you can be my friend!" said Sammy. Ned smiled and squeezed into the seat next to Sammy.

At school as the balls filed into their classroom, Sammy got stuck in the doorway! "Come on, big boy! Move it!" cried three strange-looking balls with frayed seams and scuff marks on their faces. It was the **FOUL BALL GANG**. Sammy couldn't move.

"I'm trying!" cried Sammy, but before he could get through, the Foul Ball Gang started pushing Sammy as hard as they could.

"Hey!" cried Ned. "Stop pushing Sammy!" The Foul Ball Gang turned their heads slowly toward Ned. Their faces looked mean. Just then the teacher came and helped Sammy through the doorway and made sure everyone got settled in their seats.

The teacher addressed the class: "My name is Mrs. Pitch. Would anyone like to volunteer to come up and tell the class what you like to do in your spare time? I'll write it on the board."

Connie Curveball volunteered first. She spun down the aisle between the rows of seats and curved to the board. "I'm **CONNIE CURVEBALL** and I love to dance. I brought my ballet shoes to school to show everyone."

Sammy went next. He lumbered up to the board. Each heavy step caused the balls on either side of him to bounce off their seats with surprised expressions. "I'm **SAMMY SOFTBALL** and I like to JUMP!" Then Sammy jumped up and landed with a loud *BOOM!* It made all the desks in the room jump up, too!

After seeing his friend Sammy go, Ned got up and wobbled down the aisle. The Foul Ball Gang snickered at him as he bumped and knocked books off the desks. He said in a soft voice, "My name is Ned and I love to read."

Someone from the back of the class called out, "He stumbles and bumbles! What kind of ball is he, anyway?" One of the Foul Ball Gang said, "A knucklehead ball!" and the Foul Ball Gang boys all laughed.

As Ned walked back to his seat, the three Foul Ball Gang boys each tried to trip him. But, suddenly, without even realizing what he was doing, Ned floated gracefully over each of their outstretched legs and glided into his seat.

"Hey," whispered Sammy, "how did you do that?"
Ned just smiled a secret smile.

When the bell rang for recess, the Foul Ball Gang pushed their way out, rudely bumping all the other balls aside.

Sammy, Ned, and Connie went out the front door together. Connie carried her ballet shoes.

"Don't let the Foul Ball Gang get you down, Ned," said Connie. "They're just plain mean. I think the way you move is really cool!"

"Thanks!" said Ned.

Connie put on her ballet shoes and began to pirouette. Just then the Foul Ball Gang swooped by and snatched her street shoes!

"Hey!" cried Connie, Ned, and Sammy. They gave chase, but they were too slow to catch the fast-moving Foul Ball Gang, who threw the shoes into the branches of a tree.

The three friends looked up forlornly at the shoes dangling from a high branch as the other students gathered around them and looked up, too.

"I have an idea!" shouted Sammy. "If someone sits on the seesaw, I'll jump on the other end and launch them toward the shoes!"

"I'll do it!" said **FLETCHER FASTBALL**.

"YAY! FLETCHER!" shouted all the balls.
"Let Fletcher do it! He's the fastest ball in class!"

Sammy jumped on the seesaw with a *BOOM!* and launched Fletcher like a rocket toward the shoes!

All the balls gasped as Fletcher ricocheted like a pinball off the branches and crashed to the ground in a daze.

"I'll try!" cried **FIONA FASTBALL**. "I fly straight and high!"
Sammy jumped again with a *BOOM!* onto the seesaw and launched
Fiona high into the tree. Fiona kept going up and up, until she
broke through the window of a second-floor classroom!

Everyone except the Foul Ball Gang stared in horror.
They bent over laughing and slapped each other on the back.

Ned looked up at the branches of the tree and quietly said,
"I can do it."

Sammy and Connie looked at each other and asked,
"Are you SURE?" The other balls turned to Ned with surprise.

Fletcher and Fiona, still woozy, shouted, "Don't do it, Ned!"

Ned sat on the seesaw with a determined expression as all the other balls looked at him with trepidation.

Sammy jumped up and landed once more with a **BOOM!** on the seesaw, launching Ned toward the shoes.

"Look!" shouted Sammy.
"He's not spinning!
He can get there, I know it!"

All the balls gasped. They oohed and ahhed as Ned floated
through the branches, turning this way and that. As Ned passed
the shoes, he grabbed them with a triumphant smile.

Ned descended onto the Foul Ball Gang below. He
knew exactly how he was going to land without crashing.
He bounced off each Foul Ball Gang's head and then
floated softly to the ground.

"Ned! I know about balls like you," cried Connie. "You're a knuckleball!"

"A knuckleball!" everyone exclaimed. "Knuckleballs don't spin!"

Ned smiled at Connie and Sammy. "You can't see where you're going if you're spinning too fast!"

When they got into the classroom Connie gasped and pointed at the board where the word "Knucklehead" had been written before "Ned." All the balls looked at Ned to see how he would react.

Ned confidently wove through the students to the board and erased "Knucklehead Ned." Then he wrote "**KNUCKLEBALL NED**." Everyone cheered.

Knuckleball → Sam Connie Ned

Ned smiled and said, "I love being a **KNUCKLEBALL!**"